MW01097669

First Printing, 2020

Library of Congress Control Number: 2020921874

ISBN 978-1-7361777-0-9

This book belongs to:

_____

Hello, my name is Yazmin and I am really excited about school today! My class is learning about being fair and I get to be the classroom helper.

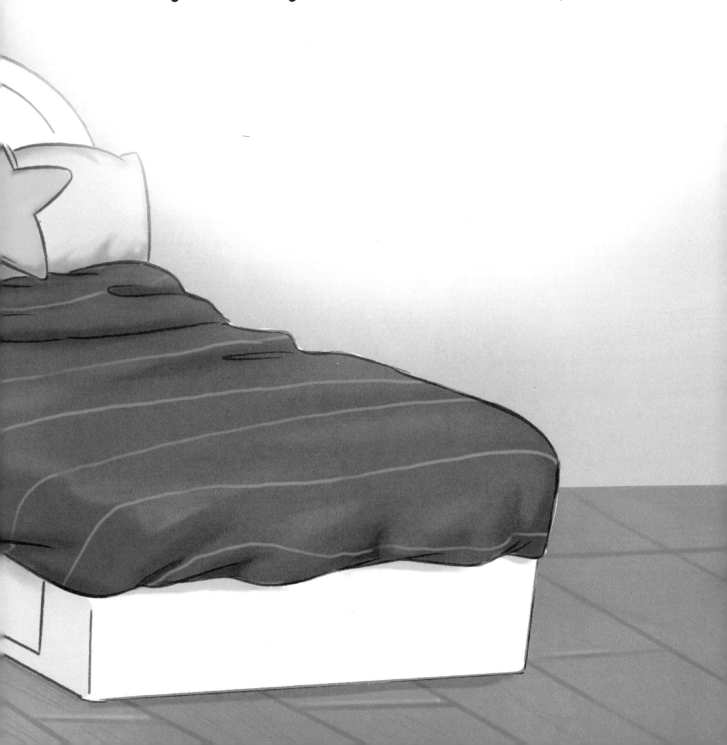

My mommy and daddy taught me how to be fair.
"Being fair does not mean everyone gets the same exact toys,
food, or clothes," Mommy said.

"Being fair is when all kids get the tools that they need
to have a good day at school," Daddy added.

My daddy is so silly. I told him that there are no tools at school,
just tables, books, blankets, headphones, and computers.
Oh yeah, and healthy food!

"Good morning Yazmin, are you ready to be the classroom helper today?" Mr. Walker asked.

"Yes, I am ready."

Equity is
Everyone's Work

"Class, can anyone tell me what we are learning today?"
Mr. Walker asked.

"Fairness!" everyone yelled.

"Yes," he replied. "We will learn about being fair but
first, everyone must wash their hands before breakfast."

"Would it be fair to give everyone a slice of peanut butter toast?" Mr. Walker asked during breakfast.

"Yes, that is fair because we all get the same thing!" Shawn replied.

"No, that is not fair because peanut butter makes Lexie sick," Yazmin said.

"If you give us all the same thing, then Lexie cannot eat breakfast and she will be hungry at school today."

"Yazmin, you are right." Said Mr. Walker. "Lexie is allergic to peanut butter, so it would not be fair to give her the same thing as the rest of the class."

"Would it be fair to give Lexie applesauce and crackers for breakfast?" Mr. Walker asked.

The entire class yelled "YES, that is fair! And fair is fair, isn't it?"

During computer time Mr. Walker passed out the headphones to each student. He asked, "is that fair?"

"Yes, that is fair because we all get headphones," Lexie explained.

"No, that is not fair because Kevin has special ears, so he needs his special device to hear the computer," Yazmin said.

"If we all get the same headphones, then Kevin will not be able to hear his lesson."

"Right, Yazmin," praised Mr. Walker. "Kevin has cochlear implants to help him hear. Class, would it be fair to give Kevin a different set of earphones for his cochlear implants?"

"Yes, that is fair. And fair is fair, isn't it?" The class yelled.

At storytime Mr. Walker told everyone to put the toys away and to have a seat. When everyone sat down, Mr. Walker asked, "is that fair?"

Elan stated, "yes, we all have to sit in a circle with no toys."

"No," Yazmin disagreed. "That is not fair because Shawn has a special blanket that helps him sit during storytime. If he does not have his blanket, then he cannot focus on the story."

YES!

"You are right, Yazmin." Mr. Walker replied. "Shawn has a weighted blanket that he uses as a tool to help him focus.

Class, would it be fair to allow Shawn to be the only student to have a blanket at storytime?"

"Yes, that is fair. And fair is fair, isn't it?" The class yelled.

After the story, Mr. Walker asked the class to share what they learned today.

Kevin smiled, "fairness does not always mean that everyone gets the same exact thing.

Like me, I need an audio cable to hear our lessons on the computer. It would not be fair to give me headphones like everyone else."

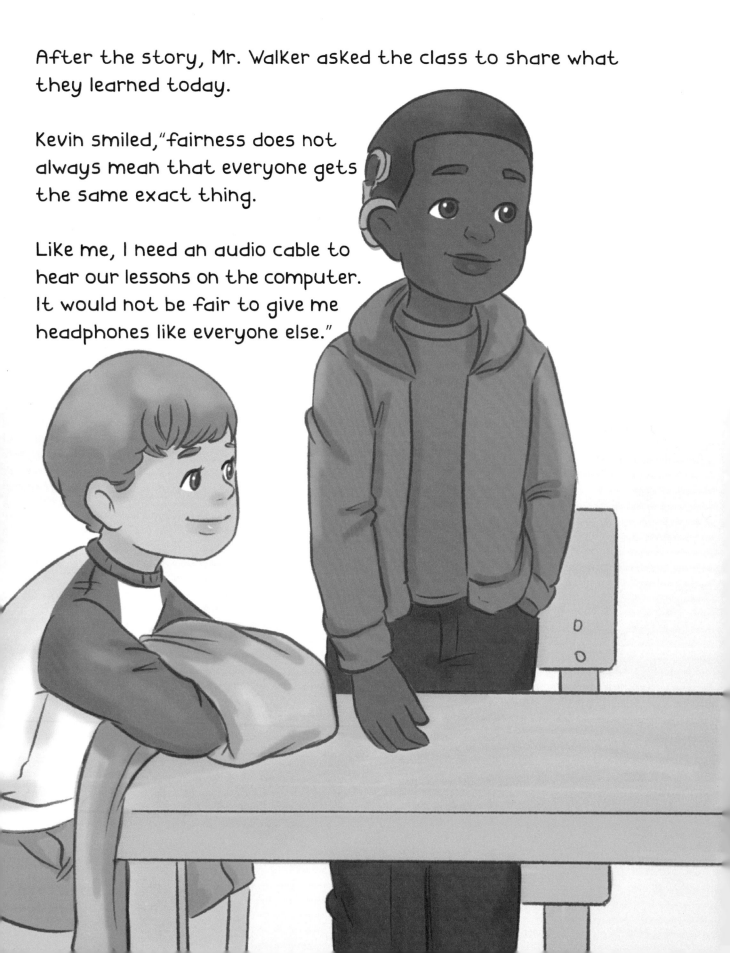

"Or me," Lexie sighed. "I get really sick when I eat peanut butter, so it would not be FAIR if you gave everyone peanut butter!"

Elaine said, "fairness may seem like a friend gets a different toy, but it may be their tool to help them have a good day."

"Like for me," Shawn said. "I get to use my weighted blanket as a tool during circle time to help me focus."

"Awesome job today, class," Mr. Walker said.
"I am really proud of each of you!

Today we learned that FAIR IS FAIR."

And the entire class yelled, "ISN'T IT?"

"What did you learn at school today?" Yamzin's dad asked.

"I learned that my classroom does have tools that help my friends have a good day. Kevin's audio cables are his tools, so that he can hear during computer time.

Lexie cannot have peanut butter so applesauce was her tool, and Shawn's weighted blanket is his tool to help him focus."

"Daddy, you were right, but what is my tool?"

CPSIA information can be obtained
at www.ICGtesting.com
Printed in the USA
LVRC090746131222
735023LV00035B/90